For Dorcas
L.J.

For Mum and Dad
T.W.

Published in 1995 by Magi Publications
55 Crowland Avenue, Hayes, Middlesex UB3 4JP

Text © 1995 by Linda Jennings
Illustrations © 1995 by Tim Warnes

Printed and bound in Italy by Grafiche AZ, Verona

ISBN 1 85430 279 5

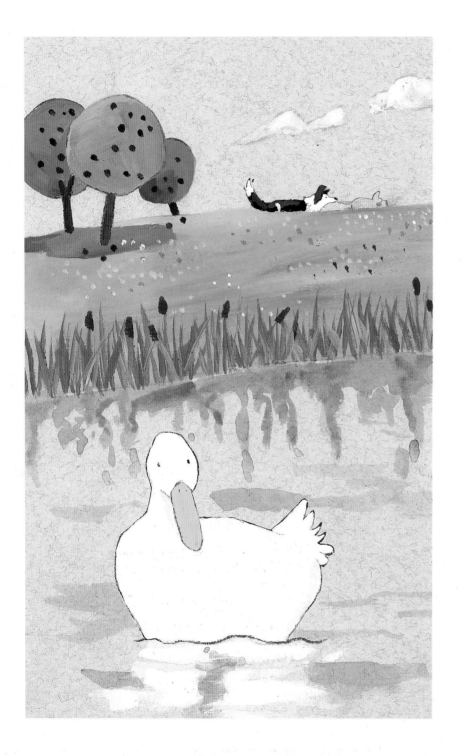

TOM'S TAIL

by
Linda Jennings

illustrated by
Tim Warnes

MAGI PUBLICATIONS
London

Tom's tail was curly like a rolled-up rubber band.
It was a very neat little tail for a piglet –
if you liked that sort of thing.
But Tom thought his tail looked silly.

In all other ways Tom was a proper little pig.

He was a nice pale pink with dirty patches here and there, where he had wallowed in mud. He slurped and snuffled in the pig-trough with all his brothers and sisters and made the usual piggy noises. But how he wished he had a straight tail!

Sam the sheepdog had
a lovely black,
plumy tail.

Hannibal the horse
had a long, swishy tail.

And Geraldine the Jersey cow had a thin, stringy tail with a little tuft on the end.

"Even the rat's tail is nicer than mine," said Tom miserably.

Very soon all the animals on
Appletree Farm were fed-up
with Tom's complaints.
"Why don't you get the tail
straightened?" said Hannibal.
"How?" asked Tom.
"Like this," said Hannibal,
and he put his big hoof on
the edge of Tom's tail.
        "Now walk away,"
        he said.

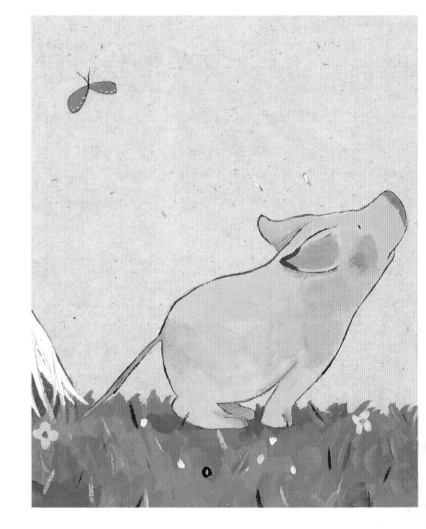

Tom squealed and squeaked
with the pain of Hannibal's
heavy hoof. But then, as he
began to walk . . .

. . . his tail stretched out,
and, when it had uncurled to
the very end, Hannibal let go . . .

PING!

Back sprang the tail . . .

. . . and Tom hurtled forward . . .

"OUCH!" yelled Tom and Sam the sheepdog together.

"Tell you what," said Sam, picking himself up.
"Why don't I take hold of your tail, and you can lead
me along. That should straighten it!"
So Tom took Sam for a walk, past the pigsties . . .

. . . round the pond . . .

. . . and over the buttercup
meadows. Very soon Tom's tail
ached and ached.
"Let go!" he cried . . .

PING!

Back sprang the tail to its usual curly-twirly self.
Tom felt miserable.

Geraldine the Jersey cow
looked at Tom, and chewed
thoughtfully.
Suddenly she had a
VERY GOOD IDEA.
She told it
to Sam . . .

. . . who took hold of Tom's tail again and stretched it.
It hurt terribly.
Then he pushed the tail into a big patch of gooey,
squelchy mud!

He made Tom lie with his tail covered
in mud for an awfully
long time, until . . .

. . . the mud dried and Tom's tail was set into a long, thin pencil.
"YIPPEE!" cried Tom.

He twirled around, trying to see his new, straight tail.
"OUCH!" said Sam.
Tom had poked him right in the chest!

"You don't half look silly," said Tom's mother.
But Tom didn't care. He liked being different.
"I'll try to wag my tail like Sam does," he said.
WHACK! The tail hit Tom's sister in the face and then
prodded his brother in the bottom.
"STOP THAT!" cried Tom's mother.

When it was dark, Tom's mother
gathered in all her piglets for
the night. They liked to
snuggle up in a big
piggy heap.
But Tom's tail got
in the way.

"GO AWAY!" cried all his brothers and sisters,
and they chased Tom right out of the sty.

Poor Tom! He tried to curl up against the farmyard wall,
but it wasn't very comfortable to lie down with a tail
as stiff as a pencil.
At long last, though, he fell asleep.

In the night it began to rain,
but Tom went on sleeping.

And as it rained, the hard mud
softened and slid off his tail.

By the time morning came, his tail was as curly-twirly as it had ever been. Grunting happily, Tom went back to the sty.

"Who wants a straight tail, anyway," said Tom later,
as he pushed and shoved into the trough with
all his brothers and sisters.

"Now if I had a long, elegant nose like Hannibal the horse instead of this silly snout, I could *really* get at the food!"